CORK & FUZZ

The Collectors

A Puffin Easy-to-Read

by **Dori Chaconas**

illustrated by **Lisa McCue**

(3817/ma)

PUFFIN BOOKS
An Imprint of Penguin Group (USA) Inc.

PUFFIN BOOKS
Published by the Penguin Group
Penguin Young Readers Group, 345 Hudson Street, New York, New York 10014, U.S.A.
Penguin Group (Canada), 90 Eglinton Avenue East, Suite 700, Toronto, Ontario,
Canada M4P 2Y3 (a division of Pearson Penguin Canada Inc.)
Penguin Books Ltd, 80 Strand, London WC2R 0RL, England
Penguin Ireland, 25 St Stephen's Green, Dublin 2, Ireland
(a division of Penguin Books Ltd)
Penguin Group (Australia), 250 Camberwell Road, Camberwell, Victoria 3124, Australia
(a division of Pearson Australia Group Pty Ltd)
Penguin Books India Pvt Ltd, 11 Community Centre,
Panchsheel Park, New Delhi - 110 017, India
Penguin Group (NZ), 67 Apollo Drive, Rosedale, North Shore 0632, New Zealand
(a division of Pearson New Zealand Ltd.)
Penguin Books (South Africa) (Pty) Ltd, 24 Sturdee Avenue,
Rosebank, Johannesburg 2196, South Africa

Registered Offices: Penguin Books Ltd, 80 Strand, London WC2R 0RL, England

First published in the United States of America by Viking,
a division of Penguin Young Readers Group, 2008
Published by Puffin Books, a division of Penguin Young Readers Group, 2010

1 3 5 7 9 10 8 6 4 2

THE LIBRARY OF CONGRESS HAS CATALOGED THE VIKING EDITION AS FOLLOWS:
Chaconas, Dori, date–
Cork and Fuzz : the collectors / by Dori Chaconas ; illustrated by Lisa McCue.
p. cm.
Summary: When best friends Cork and Fuzz go to the pond to collect shiny stones,
they happen upon a duck's nest just as the eggs are hatching and Fuzz,
who is wearing a feather from his collection, is collected by the mother duck.
ISBN: 978-0-670-06286-7 (hardcover)
[1. Collectors and collecting—Fiction. 2. Best friends—Fiction. 3. Opossums—Fiction.
4. Muskrat—Fiction. 5. Ducks—Fiction. 6. Friendship—Fiction.]
I. McCue, Lisa, ill. II. Title. III. Title: Cork and Fuzz.
PZ7.C342Cot 2008 [E]—dc22 2007017900

Puffin® and Easy-to-Read® are registered trademarks of Penguin Group (USA) Inc.

Puffin Books ISBN 978-0-14-241714-0

Manufactured in China
Set in Bookman

Chapter One

Cork was a short muskrat. He collected shiny stones.

Fuzz was a tall possum. He collected shiny stones,

empty lunch bags, bottle caps,

pinecones,

long sticks,

gum wrappers,

food,

and more food.

Two collectors. Two best friends.

Cork ran to Fuzz's house. Fuzz was in his yard. He held a long feather with his tail. Fuzz swept his tail back and forth.

"You look like a bird," Cork said.

"I am sweeping leaves," said Fuzz. "I am looking for shiny stones to collect. I cannot see them if the leaves are on top."

"I will help!" Cork said. "You sweep. I will

walk behind you and look."

Fuzz swept.

Sweep! Sweep! Swip!

"Yah-hee!" Cork laughed.

"Are you laughing at me?" Fuzz asked.

"I am not laughing at you," Cork said.

"Your feather tickled my chin."

Fuzz swept again.

Sweep! Sweep! Swip!

"Ka-chee! *Ka-chee!*" Cork sneezed.

"Are you sneezing at me?" Fuzz asked.

"I am not sneezing at you," Cork said.

"Your feather tickled my nose."

"Did you find any shiny stones?" Fuzz asked.

"No," said Cork.

"Nuts!" Fuzz said.

"I do not think there are any shiny stones here at all," Cork said. "Have you ever found a shiny stone in your yard?"

"Nope," said Fuzz. "Mostly I just find dirt."

"Nuts," said Cork.

Chapter Two

"We could go to my pond," Cork said.

"We can collect lots of stones there."

"Okay!" said Fuzz.

"Are you going to throw that feather away?"
Cork asked.

"No," Fuzz said. "I am collecting feathers, too."

"You collect too many things," Cork said.

"You just say that because I thought of collecting
feathers first," Fuzz said.

"That is not true," said Cork.

"You just say that because you do not have a
feather," Fuzz said.

"That is not true," said Cork.

"Maybe we will find a feather for you," Fuzz said.

"Really?" said Cork. "That would be very nice."

At the pond, Cork and Fuzz looked for feathers
in the ferns. They looked for stones in the reeds.

"Cork!" Fuzz yelled. "I found some green stones!
They are very pretty!"

Cork looked.

14

"I do not think they are stones," he said.

Fuzz picked one up.

CRACK!

"Uh-oh!" Fuzz said. "This stone just cracked."

CRACK! CRACK! CRACK!

"Uh-oh!" Cork said. "All the stones are cracking!
There is something inside!"

"Peep! Peep! Peep!"

"Maybe they are baby buzzard bees!" Fuzz said.

"Peep! Peep! Peep!"

The ducklings popped out of their shells.

They ran to Fuzz.

"They see your feather," Cork said. "They think

you are their mother."

"Really?" Fuzz said. "I will collect baby buzzard bees!"

"You collect too many things," Cork said.

He put the ducklings back in the nest.

"Peep! Peep! Peep!"

Pop! Pop! Pop!

"Maybe they are baby grass-poppers," Fuzz said. "You put them in. They pop back out."

Fuzz helped Cork put the ducklings back in the nest again.

"Peep! Peep! Peep!"

Pop! Pop! Pop!

"QUACK! QUACK! QUACK!"

Fuzz yelled, "Run for your life!

It is the mother buzzard bee!"

Chapter Three

Cork ran one way.

Fuzz ran the other way.

The ducklings ran every which way.

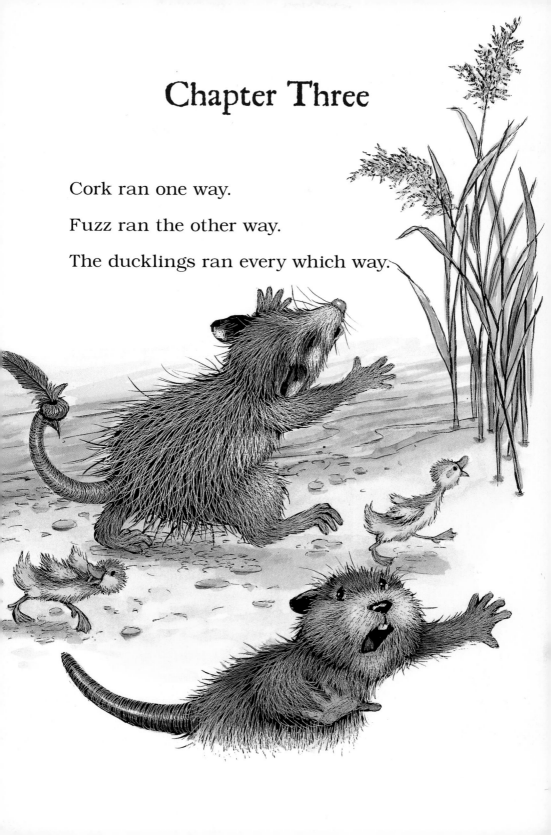

Cork found Fuzz hiding in the reeds.

"Do you think she will find us?" Fuzz whispered.

"Shhh!" said Cork.

"What will she do to us?" Fuzz whispered.

"Shhh!" said Cork.

"Peep! Peep! Peep!"

"Uh-oh!" Cork said. "The babies found you."

"Shhh!" Fuzz whispered to the ducklings. "Go away, or the mother buzzard bee will find us!"

"Peep! Peep! Peep! Peep! Peep!"

"QUACK!"

"Nuts!" Fuzz said. "She found us."

"*Quack!*"

The mother duck pecked one duckling on

the tail. The duckling ran back to the nest.

"*Quack! Quack! Quack!*"

She pecked the other ducklings on their

tails. They ran back to the nest.

"*QUACK!*" She pecked Fuzz on the tail.

"Help!" Fuzz said. "She is collecting me!"

"She sees your feather," Cork said. "She thinks you are her baby!"

"What should I do?" Fuzz asked.

"Throw the feather away," Cork said.

"No!" said Fuzz. "I am collecting feathers!"

The mother duck pushed Fuzz to the nest.

She sat on the ducklings.

And she sat on Fuzz.

Cork crept up behind the nest.

"Fuzz!" he whispered. "I will get you out of there."

"Why?" asked Fuzz. "It is very nice here. The mother buzzard bee is soft and warm."

Cork scratched his head.

"Well," he said. "If you stay there, can I have all your collections?"

"Cork!" Fuzz said. "I need my collections!

Get me out of here!"

"I will think of something," Cork whispered.

Chapter Four

Cork crawled away. He sat in a fern patch.

Think . . . think . . . think! he thought.

He picked a fern. He tied it to his tail. He picked two more ferns. He tied them to his arms.

"I will scare the big quacker," Cork said. "I will make her run away. Then I will save Fuzz."

He flapped back to the nest.

"Cork?" Fuzz asked. "Is that you?"

"I AM NOT CORK," Cork said in a big voice.

"I AM A GIANT CORK BIRD! *CORK! CORK!*"

The mother duck looked surprised. But she did

not look scared. She laughed, *"Qua! Qua! Qua!"*

Cork flapped his fern wings.

The mother duck laughed harder.

"*QUA-QUA-QUA-QUA-QUA!*"

She laughed so hard she fell off the nest.

Cork grabbed Fuzz. They ran far away from the ducks.

"Do you know why I like you?" Fuzz asked. "Because you look after me. You saved me from the giant buzzard bee!"

"I do not think it was a buzzard bee," Cork said. "It did not buzz. It quacked. It was a duck."

"Then you saved me from the giant quacker duck," Fuzz said.

He took his paw from behind his back. He handed Cork a feather.

"Oooooo!" Cork said.

"It was in the quacker duck's nest," said Fuzz. "Now you can collect feathers, too."

"Do you know why I like you?" Cork said. "Because you make me feel good in my heart. And you always make me laugh."

"Like this?" Fuzz asked. Then he said in a big voice, "I AM NOT FUZZ! I AM A GIANT QUACKER DUCK! You are a baby quacker duck! I will sit on you!"

Fuzz chased Cork. They ran and they
flapped and they quacked.
Two best friends,
collecting laughs all the way home.